Mona's Magic Trick

T0337188

Written by Katie Foufouti

Illustrated by Valentina Pieralli

Collins

What's in this story?

Listen and say 🎧①

theatre

wand

Download the audio at www.collins.co.uk/839780

magician

magic trick

Mona likes learning magic tricks.
She got a new book for her birthday.
It says *Lisa's Tricks for Children*.
Lisa is Mona's favourite magician.

Mona would like to be a magician.
She does magic tricks every day.

She always does tricks for her brother, Alfie.

Mona asks, "Can you see this wand, Alfie? Now, are you watching? Where's the wand? It's magic!"

Alfie laughs.

Mona asks, "Why are you laughing?"

Alfie understands the trick. He says,
"The wand is behind your arm, Mona,
I saw you hide it. Can you do it faster?"

On Friday, Mona is shopping with her dad in the supermarket. She sees a poster.

LISA, the best magician in the world!

Look! It's Lisa the magician!

At home, Mona's dad looks on
the computer. He buys two tickets to see
Lisa on Sunday. Mona's very happy.

Mona says, "Lisa is the best!"

It's the big day. Mona and her dad go to see Lisa. There are lots of people at the theatre.

A boy is standing in front of Mona. His name is Josh. Josh knows a trick and he shows it to Mona. Mona shows him a trick, too.

In the theatre, Josh claps and Mona shouts. They want to see Lisa the magician.

A man comes on. He says, "Hello, children and parents! Welcome to the theatre. Here's Lisa, the best magician in the world!"

Lisa takes a long, red scarf from her coat.
She holds it up, then she waves it up
and down.

Now the scarf is a wand!

Mona says, "What a great trick!"

Lisa needs help for her next trick.
Lisa and Josh both put up their hands.

15

She chooses Mona *and* Josh! They both run up.

They say, "Hello, Lisa!"

Lisa has got a bucket.

Lisa asks Josh, "Have you got any coins?"

Josh says, "No, I haven't."

Lisa says, "Let's see …" She takes two coins from Josh's nose!

Lisa asks, "Where are your coins?
Show me your hands."

Three coins fall in the bucket!

Lisa says, "Thank you, Mona. Thank you, Josh! Here you are – a coin for you."

Before Mona sits down, she wants to do a trick, too.

Mona says, "Look, Lisa. I can do a trick with a coin, too."

The coin isn't in her hand! Where is it?

Lisa says, "Well done, Mona!
You're a magician!"

Everyone claps. What a fantastic day!

Picture dictionary

Listen and repeat

bucket

coin

poster

scarf

shout

ticket

world

1 Look and order the story

2 Listen and say

Collins

Published by Collins
An imprint of HarperCollins*Publishers*
Westerhill Road
Bishopbriggs
Glasgow
G64 2QT

HarperCollins*Publishers*
1st Floor, Watermarque Building
Ringsend Road
Dublin 4
Ireland

William Collins' dream of knowledge for all began with the publication of his first book in 1819.

A self-educated mill worker, he not only enriched millions of lives, but also founded a flourishing publishing house. Today, staying true to this spirit, Collins books are packed with inspiration, innovation and practical expertise. They place you at the centre of a world of possibility and give you exactly what you need to explore it.

© HarperCollins*Publishers* Limited 2020

10 9 8 7 6 5 4 3 2

ISBN 978-0-00-839780-7

Collins® and COBUILD® are registered trademarks of HarperCollins*Publishers* Limited

www.collins.co.uk/elt

British Library Cataloguing in Publication Data

A catalogue record for this publication is available from the British Library.

Author: Katie Foufouti
Illustrator: Valentina Pieralli (Beehive)
Series editor: Rebecca Adlard
Commissioning editor: Fiona Undrill
Publishing manager: Lisa Todd
Product managers: Jennifer Hall and Caroline Green
In-house editor: Alma Puts Keren
Project manager: Emily Hooton
Editor: Emma Wilkinson
Proofreaders: Natalie Murray and Michael Lamb
Cover designer: Kevin Robbins
Typesetter: 2Hoots Publishing Services Ltd
Audio produced by id audio, London
Reading guide author: Emma Wilkinson
Production controller: Rachel Weaver
Printed and bound by: GPS Group, Slovenia

MIX
Paper from responsible sources

FSC
www.fsc.org

FSC™ C007454

Download the audio for this book and a reading guide for parents and teachers at www.collins.co.uk/839780